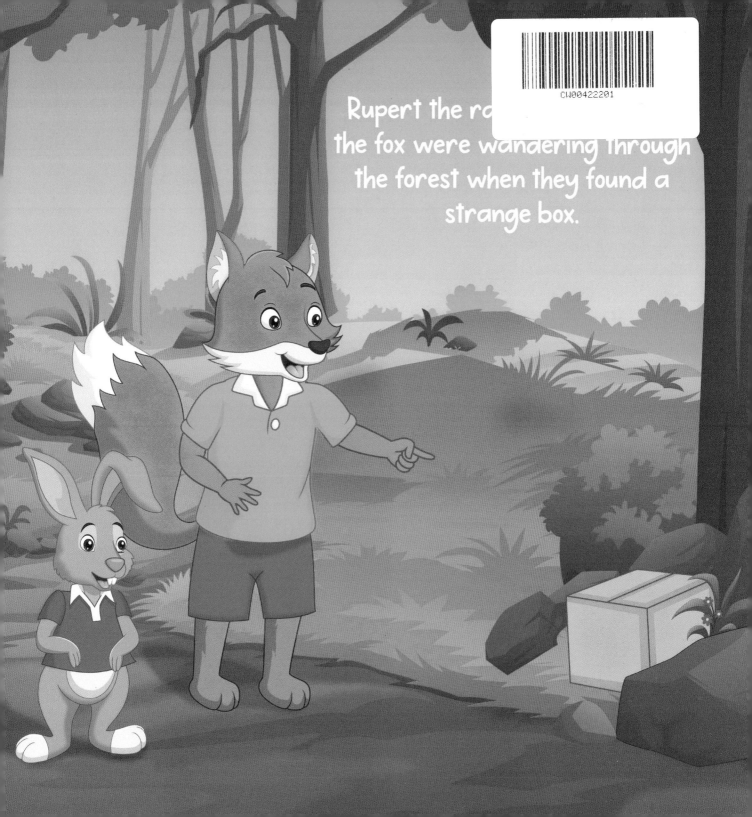

Rupert the ra... the fox were wandering through the forest when they found a strange box.

Rupert was scared but Francis was not.
When they opened the box you wouldn't
believe what they got.

Rupert rubbed his eyes with excitement and glee!
Inside the box was a map, where will it lead?

They hurried to tell their friend Daisy the deer

She looked at the map with joy and cheer!

They started the adventure the very next day.
They were walking along the trail and that's when they say!

Oh no a river so long and so wide,
How will they get to the other side?

They look along the river and can see a friendly frog

When they ask for help, He says to cross at the big log

When they were crossing the log it started to shake

Then they began to run, scared it might break

A hop and a jump and they landed on a rock.

They all got to the other side to continue their walk.

They travelled through the forest deep into the night
But that's when they came across a mountain, tall in height.

Its too tall to climb and too big to walk around
They were all out of hope and that's when they found...

An Owl named Otis who knew what to do.
There was a cave in the mountain that
they could go through

The cave was dark and Rupert could barely see where he was going.

But Otis could see the path at the end was showing.

Rupert, was fast Francis was too
But Daisy was behind she struggled to get through,
She eventually managed to squeeze through the gap.
She jumped out the cave and continued to follow the map!

Rupert and the gang carried on
following the trail.

With the map in their hands they
were determined not to fail!

Confidence
is my
Superpower

Alicia Ortego

Then they bumped into a badger who was blocking the track.

The badger said "I have dug a big hole, if you continue you will not come back"

Francis said to the gang "what should we do?"
Rupert replied "we must carry on i'll keep a good view"

They followed the path being extra careful.
Rupert and his friends needed to be successful.

Rupert spotted a hole covered in leaves and branches.
They decide to jump and take their chances.

Rupert and Daisy get across no problem at all.
But Francis is behind, he looks like he might fall.

Francis tries to jump but slips in the mud.

Rupert and Daisy thought he fell because they heard a big thud!

Francis just managed to jump over the trap
He was so happy that he could continue to
follow the map

They travelled through the night until
the early morning
The group stuck together
searching and exploring

The birds in the forest were chirping
and singing
Rupert and his friends were chatting
and grinning

Rupert shouted with excitement
'Look I see the box, its up ahead"

They ran to the box "I wonder
what's inside" Daisy said

When they looked at the box it was shining and glowing

The moment they opened it up you won't believe what it was showing...

Inside was a letter old and crinkled

As they read it their eyes grew large and twinkled

The letter talked about the journey they had been on and places they had seen

And if you work together with your friends you can achieve your dreams

Rupert and his friends realised that the adventure they had been on together,

was more important than a prize, they had made memories that will last forever.

THE END

Fraser Ryan

Printed in Great Britain
by Amazon

82409097R00016